THE STONE MOUSE

"The book is written in a direct and unsentimental style that is a pleasure to read. Helen Craig's drawings are finely tuned to the story and beautifully executed." *The Times Educational Supplement*

Jenny Nimmo worked at the BBC for a number of years, ending in a spell as a director/adaptor for *Jackanory*. Her many books for children include *The Night of the Unicorn*, *Ronnie and the Giant Millipede*, *The Stone Mouse* (highly commended for the Carnegie Medal and broadcast on BBC TV), *The Owl-tree* (winner of the Smarties Book Prize), *Toby in the Dark*, *Dog Star* and *Tom and the Pterosaur*. Her well-known trilogy, comprising *The Snow Spider* (winner of the Smarties Book Prize), *Emlyn's Moon* and *The Chestnut Soldier* has been made into a television series. Jenny lives in a converted watermill in Wales with her artist husband and occasionally her three grown-up children.

Helen Craig has been writing and illustrating children's books for thirty years, and has countless titles to her name, including her retelling of *The Town Mouse and the Country Mouse* (shortlisted for the Smarties Book Prize) and its sequel, *Charlie and Tyler at the Seaside*; four *This Is the Bear* books and *Mary, Mary*, all written by Sarah Hayes; four Bonnie Bumble books, by Phyllis Root; and the hugely popular stories about Angelina Ballerina, broadcast on TV. Helen lives in London.

A flight of narrow steps wound down to a shining stretch of sand and the ocean.

THE
STONE MOUSE

Written by
JENNY NIMMO

Illustrated by
HELEN CRAIG

WALKER BOOKS
AND SUBSIDIARIES

LONDON • BOSTON • SYDNEY • AUCKLAND

For Gina and Murray
J.N.

First published 1993 by Walker Books Ltd
87 Vauxhall Walk, London SE11 5HJ

This edition published 2004

2 4 6 8 10 9 7 5 3

Text © 1993 Jenny Nimmo
Illustrations © 1993 Helen Craig Ltd

The right of Jenny Nimmo and Helen Craig
to be identified as author and illustrator respectively of this
work has been asserted by them in accordance with the
Copyright, Designs and Patents Act 1988

This book has been typeset in Plantin Light

Printed in Great Britain by J.H. Haynes & Co. Ltd

British Library Cataloguing in Publication Data:
a catalogue record for this book is
available from the British Library

ISBN 1-84428-632-0

www.walkerbooks.co.uk

CONTENTS

The stone mouse watched Aunt Maria walk to her front door.

CHAPTER ONE

"Take care of the family, Stone Mouse," said Aunt Maria. She zipped up her travelling bag, put on her soft black hat and then touched his head, very gently. "You won't be lonely," she told him. "The children will talk to you."

The stone mouse watched Aunt Maria walk to her front door. She had to use a stick these days because her legs let her down, sometimes, and she often stumbled up the narrow step to her kitchen. Through the open door the stone mouse caught a glimpse of the taxi that would whisk Aunt Maria away.

And then he was alone.

He sat on the polished hall table between a notebook and a telephone, where the family were bound to see him when they arrived. He listened to the seagulls, to passing cars and footsteps. No one came to Aunt Maria's door.

A gloomy darkness crept into the house and soon the only sound was the distant murmur of the sea. The stone mouse wondered if he would be alone all night but then the *rat-tap* of the cat flap told him that Moss and Minnie had come in. The two cats passed him on their way to the kitchen. They glanced up at the mouse in a friendly way; they only hunted running mice.

It was such a very long night. The stone mouse closed his eyes and dreamed of being carried in Aunt Maria's deep pocket. Sleep always led him to this memory. He supposed that before Aunt Maria found him he had only been a slumbering stone without any thoughts. The old woman had woken him up and given him a name. "Mouse." It suited him perfectly.

Sunlight swept across the stone mouse. Alert and eager, he listened to the bangs and slams of a family car. Someone ran towards the house, two more followed at a slower pace. A key turned and a man strode through the door carrying suitcases, then came a woman with an anxious face and bags of different sizes hanging from her arms. Behind her a boy shuffled, biting his lip and looking angry.

They stopped beside the stone mouse, their shadows covering him. They littered the table where he sat, with keys and comics and scraps of sticky paper, and none of them spoke to the stone mouse or even seemed to notice him. They bustled on into the house and he could hear them, feeding the cats and finding the cups and a kettle. A jumble of voices rang out from the kitchen.

"Ted, put that down!" "Mind the cats!" "Where's Elly?"

The boy ran through the hall again and leapt up the stairs, shouting about the bedroom he hoped for, where there was plenty of space to play.

The stone mouse felt his welcoming smile begin to fade. They can't see me, he thought. They don't need me. Perhaps I'm not a mouse at all and Aunt Maria's chatter wasn't really meant for me. The stone mouse felt a little knife of ice strike through him. The cold crept right into his tiny feet and ears and froze them. He was terribly afraid that he might be turning back into a stone again.

He looked through the open door to get one last view of the sky before it was too late. Already his picture of the world was getting blurred.

And then a girl came into the house. She came right up to the mouse and putting out her hand said, "Oh, a stone mouse!"

When she smiled the stone mouse knew that his soft coat, his ears, eyes and whiskers were all in place, and that his heart was beating.

*"It's a dirty old pebble," said Ted, sliding
down the banisters.*

CHAPTER TWO

"It's a dirty old pebble," said Ted, sliding down the banisters.

"Ted, don't do that," said Mrs Martin, climbing past him.

"Mouse!" said Ted. "Elly's crazy."

Ted is dangerous, thought the stone mouse.

Elly scowled at her brother. Sometimes he just wasn't worth talking to. She picked up the stone mouse. He was soft and silky with bright, dark eyes and very small ears, but he had no tail at all.

"Did you lose your tail in battle?" whispered Elly, glancing at Moss and Minnie.

"Actually I never had one," the stone mouse replied. His voice was so faint, Elly had to hold him close to her ear.

"What did you say?" she asked the mouse.

"Now she's talking to a pebble," scoffed Ted. "I never knew anyone so daft."

"That's enough, Ted," said Mr Martin. "Come and help me with these bags."

Elly felt a prickle of anger. She wished Ted was someone else's brother. She wished something would make him cry for a change. She took the mouse outside and sat on the step.

"What's the matter, Elly?" said the stone mouse in a gentle voice. "You've been crying."

"How can you tell?" asked Elly, wiping her eyes.

"It's not difficult," said the mouse. "Your

eyes look sore and there's something else –
I can't quite put it into words."

"Sadness," Elly told him. "I had to leave
my dog behind."

"Dog?" The stone mouse looked carefully into Elly's troubled face.

"My birthday puppy," Elly went on,
almost to herself. "They said he'd upset
Aunt Maria's cats. He chases everything,
you see: leaves, butterflies, even bicycles…"

"And you, of course!"

"Of course," said Elly. "His name is
Sunny."

"What a rascal," said the stone mouse, in
a tone that exactly matched Aunt Maria's
when she spoke to her cats.

"Our next-door neighbour, Mrs Thorpe,
is looking after him. But he needs *me*. He'll
howl all night and probably won't eat his
dinner. He'll get ill."

The stone mouse was surprised by a very clear picture of a yellow-coloured dog with floppy ears and large paws, a carefree dog who ran beside a woman in pink trainers.

"Sunny's all right." As the mouse said this the dog in his head took flight, bounding through the grass beneath a whirling stick.

"How do you know?" Elly frowned, suspiciously.

"I know," the mouse replied. "Mrs Thorpe loves dogs and exercise, otherwise she wouldn't have taken on the job."

"I see. Well, if you're sure." Elly began to believe this truthful-looking mouse.

Her mother called from an upstairs window, "Elly, come and look at your room. Your bed's got pictures on it and you can see the ocean."

When Elly looked up, she found Ted

watching her from another window. "My room's bigger," he crowed.

"So what," said Elly, who only cared if her room had a drawer to hide things in.

She carried the stone mouse inside and laid him, carefully, on the table before she went up to find her room. He gave a little squeak of protest but it never reached Elly, who was already planning where to put her treasures: the brown rabbit, the wooden ducks and a photo of her best friend, Jane Beddoes. She hoped there was a drawer where she could hide her diary and her favourite book. Ted had a habit of teasing her about the books she read, and if he found the diary...? Elly dreaded to think what Ted would do. All her secret thoughts would be shouted about and made to look silly.

"Is there a drawer?" asked Elly, running

into the room where her mother was gazing from a window.

"Look, Elly, the sea!" said Mrs Martin.

"Yes, but is there a...?" and then Elly began to take note of all the strange and wonderful things around her: pictures made of shells, a glass dolphin, a patchwork quilt and a bedside table with a very tiny drawer.

"I like it," she said.

"I thought you would. Now come and look at the sea."

"Oooooh," sighed Elly. "It's silver, and so near."

The back garden was neatly divided by a narrow path that led to a gate, and beyond the gate a flight of narrow steps, which Elly could not yet see, wound down to a shining stretch of sand and the ocean.

"Aren't we lucky," said Mrs Martin.

Ted peered in; he still wore the angry

look that frightened Elly. "Can I go on the beach?" he said.

"After tea, Ted," his mother told him, and he went away, thumping down the stairs as though his shoes had lead in them.

"What's the matter with Ted?" Elly moved closer to her mother.

"He won't tell me."

"I wish the old Ted would come back."

Ted had reached the hall table. He glared at the stone mouse and the mouse stared bravely back. But he felt terribly afraid.

*Elly realized that no one else could
hear the mouse.*

CHAPTER THREE

Mr Martin struggled with Aunt Maria's stove. He was used to electricity and it was a long time since he'd been camping and had to use twigs and paper. He gave up the struggle and told Ted to fetch more coal from the yard.

Ted swung the scuttle, hitting the back door. "This is a stupid house," he grumbled.

Mrs Martin was trying to make the best of things. "Perhaps there's a gas ring, somewhere," she suggested. "I could heat up some baked beans."

But Mr Martin was determined. "I'll get this stove going if it kills me," he said.

Ted, crashing about with the scuttle, shouted, "It probably will."

"Ted's in such a rage," whispered Elly. "I'm afraid he's going to do something evil."

"Don't be silly, Elly," said her mother.

So Elly kept her thoughts to herself and didn't say a word when Ted came back and dumped the coal down with a bang. But she watched him, out of the corner of her eye, while pretending to draw seagulls.

Mr Martin poked the stove, threw in a firelighter and closed it. "There," he said. "That's done it."

His wife began happily arranging saucepans, singing for good measure and smiling at her children as if to say: Hot food is everything. Soon we'll all feel better.

But the stove wouldn't co-operate. It blew a gust of black smoke into their faces and then another. It hissed and grumbled but it wouldn't heat their supper. Moss and Minnie walked out of the kitchen as politely as they could and the cat flap rattled twice.

"Cats leaving a sinking ship," Mr Martin remarked, half in fun.

"Oh, really!" Mrs Martin began to give in to despair. "This can't go on. How did Aunt Maria manage?"

"Ask the stone mouse," said Elly without looking up. She could feel Ted's sneer through all her clothes.

"I'm afraid it'll take more than a mouse to get this thing going," said Mr Martin gloomily.

"Sandwiches!" Mrs Martin tried to raise her spirits. "I'll get out the ham and lettuce. We'll light the wretched stove in the morning. Someone's bound to know about these things."

"I hate sandwiches," Ted bellowed. "I need something hot. I need sausages and beans and, probably, chips. And then I want a bath. I feel dirty after that long journey. And you said we wouldn't get hot water until the stove was working. I hate this horrible, difficult, rotten place."

"Shut up, Ted!" roared Mr Martin. He pulled out a chair and flung himself into it, resting his arms on the table and his head in his hands.

Elly got up quietly and went into the hall. The stone mouse sat at attention on his table. He'd been listening to the arguments and guessed what was expected of him.

"Can you help?" asked Elly.

"I'd be very happy to try," he replied.

So she took him into the kitchen and set him on the dresser, just behind Ted, whose rage now simmered, underground. Mrs Martin had begun to hum, and while this was supposed to sooth them all it somehow made everything seem more desperate. Then into the quietness and just above the hum, the stone mouse said, "Open the flue-damper."

Elly realized that no one else could hear the mouse and she didn't know what a flue-damper was.

"If you open the damper the draught will draw the smoke up the chimney," explained the knowledgeable mouse. "I've seen Aunt Maria do it many a time. You'll have a roaring fire to heat your supper and all the hot water you could want."

Elly stared hard at her father, hoping he would understand the mouse, but he took no notice and although her mother had fallen silent, she seemed more intent on cutting ham than attending to a stone mouse.

So Elly spoke up. "Open the flue-damper!"

The mouse gave further instructions. "There's a little lever at the bottom of the chimney pipe. Just turn it forward."

Elly repeated, word for word.

Mr Martin looked up. "That'll do it," he exclaimed. "Of course, that'll do it." And he jumped up, rubbing his hands like someone who's certain he's going to win.

Elly couldn't be sure if it was her voice he had heard or the mouse's. Or maybe he was listening to a message in his head.

"Elly, you're a marvel," Mrs Martin declared. "How did you guess?"

"It was the mouse," admitted Elly. "He's seen Aunt Maria do it many a time."

"Well, well," said her mother.

The fire roared up, the smoke disappeared, the saucepans started bubbling.

"Hurray!" cheered Elly's father, swinging her round in a hug.

Proud and pleased, the stone mouse settled back to watch his happy family.

"You'll get your hot supper after all," Ted's mother told him.

"And your bath," said Elly.

"I don't want it now," Ted muttered. "My lungs are full of smoke," and he turned to glare at the stone mouse, who suddenly found he had to cling fast to his mouseness.

The battle isn't won, he thought.

A moon appeared above the water and fingers of light crept about the ocean floor.

Chapter Four

When Elly went to bed the stone mouse tried to catch her eye. "Don't leave me down here," he begged. "It's dangerous."

Elly didn't hear him because Mrs Martin was scrubbing the saucepans and Mr Martin was going on about fishing and bird-watching and visits to cliffs and lighthouses.

When Elly had gone, Ted said, "You promised I could go on the beach after supper."

Because he looked so miserable his mother couldn't refuse. "Just to the bottom of the steps, then," she said. "No further."

"Promise," said Ted, brightening up.

"And you know you don't have to worry because I've got my 100 metres swimming badge." He turned very quickly and slipped the stone mouse into his pocket.

"Help!" came the mouse's muffled cry.

Ted opened the back door and ran down the path to the steps. His mother watched him through the kitchen window. "I think he's going to be all right, after all," she told Mr Martin. "He's been so sulky all day. He wanted to do something special with that friend of his, Jon what's-his-name but, as I told him, we can't do everything we want to."

"He'll cheer up," said Mr Martin. "The sea will do it."

Ted had reached the bottom of the steps. He took the stone mouse out of his pocket but he didn't look at it. He didn't want to see the glint of a tiny eye or the stirring of a whisker. The shore sparkled with wet pebbles. Ted approached the waves.

"Don't," pleaded the stone mouse, reading the danger signals. "It won't make you feel any better."

"It will," Ted shouted in a sudden fury. He raised his arm and flung the stone mouse at the clouds.

"Elly!" called the mouse as he spun into the sky. "Help me!" But his voice was lost in the wind and drowned by the tumbling sea.

"Elly!" the mouse sighed in despair. He hit the ocean with a splash that stunned him, and dropped through the cold gloomy water without any sense of where or what he was. Though, just before he sank onto a bed of seaweed, he managed to whisper, "I'm just a stone after all."

And yet he wasn't just a stone!

A moon appeared above the water and fingers of light crept about the ocean floor, showing the mouse that he hadn't lost his mousy curiosity.

The gleaming shapes that crawled and darted all about him were talkative and friendly. Only the pebbles worried him, with their smooth, eyeless surfaces and lack of conversation. They made him sad and even more determined to be an animal.

In the middle of the night Elly woke up. Was it a sound that disturbed her? Or just the emptiness of something missing? Perhaps it was a moonbeam slipping past the curtains and alighting on her cheek.

Elly, wide awake now, swung her feet into her slippers and ran to the window. The shining sea looked cold and dangerous.

"The stone mouse," said Elly to the moon.

"He shouldn't be alone tonight." She took her torch from the bedside drawer and went downstairs to fetch the mouse. Moonlight danced everywhere. The night was like a dark, silvery day so Elly could see her way quite clearly. She could see the hall and the table with the muddle of litter that her family had left on it, but there was no stone mouse.

He *was* there, thought Elly. I know he was. So who has kidnapped him? She turned at a low sound coming from the kitchen. No one there. But, beaming her torch through the doorway, she found four tiny lights moving closer. They were a dangerous glowing green! Elly would have screamed if four sharp ears and eight white feet had not come into view. The cats purred at her in a comforting way.

"What have you done with him?" hissed Elly.

"We're innocent," mewed Minnie huffily.

"We don't eat stone mice."

"We like our mouse," Moss added. "Ted's taken him. We saw it happen."

Their trills and yowling made no sense to Elly, yet she realized that the stone mouse had been living quite happily with Moss and Minnie. No harm had come to him before.

"I'm sorry," said Elly. "I didn't mean to offend you. But where d'you think he is?" And then she remembered. "Of course, the kitchen." She leapt up the narrow kitchen steps and turned on the light.

"Not there!" said Moss, cross at being nearly trodden on.

Elly searched the dresser, pulling out drawers, lifting cups and plates, scrabbling among the cutlery.

"No! No!" mewed Minnie impatiently. "Don't human beings have any instinct about these things?"

"Elly," called an anxious voice and Mrs Martin appeared in a blue and white nightgown. "What are you doing? It's the middle of the night."

"He's gone, Mum!" cried Elly. "The stone mouse has gone. Someone's stolen him."

"Of course they haven't," said Mrs Martin, yawning. "Come to bed, Elly."

Elly couldn't leave the kitchen until she'd made quite certain the stone mouse wasn't hiding from her. And yet, as she scanned the tidy shelves, she knew, somehow, that the mouse wasn't even in the house.

"It's Ted," she said. "He's taken the mouse and put him where I'll never find him."

"If it's Ted, then it's just a game and of course he'll give him back," said Mrs Martin.

"No he won't," said Elly with certainty. She let her mother lead her back to bed but she couldn't sleep. She lay and watched light spread behind the curtains and listened to the seagulls waking. A car roared by and a train rattled in the distance, but the sea hardly whispered.

"It's not just that I miss him," Elly said to herself. "I'm afraid for him."

Back in their baskets, Moss and Minnie curled up comfortably. Fond as they were of Aunt Maria's mouse, they never allowed problems to invade their sleep. Time for all that tomorrow.

The stone mouse was very tired. The sea had pulled him off his bed and swept him round and round in an uncomfortable jig, pushing him, at last, into a little hollow filled with shells. Looking up, the mouse had seen the swirling water brighten and become so thin that he could see a cloud roll through the sky above it. The shells about him began to glisten. A frill of bubbles tickled his neck. His skin felt warm. The sea had fallen off him. Only his feet remained in a pool of water, but the rest of him was surely visible.

It's up to Elly now, the stone mouse thought.

Elly began to tiptoe across the rocks...
she was searching for a mouse.

CHAPTER FIVE

"Shall we go on the beach?" Elly asked when breakfast was over.

Ted shrugged and wouldn't answer.

"Come on," Elly pleaded.

"We'll go without him, Elly," said Mr Martin. "We don't want grouches with gloomy faces on the beach."

"It isn't gloomy," muttered Ted. "It's just an ordinary face…"

"That can't smile." Elly felt bold for a moment but immediately wished she hadn't spoken, for Ted whirled round, eyes blazing, and stormed at her, "Can smile if it wants to. But it doesn't want to. Get it?"

"Get it," said Elly, moving swiftly behind her father.

All the same, Ted followed them onto the beach. Trailing his spade with a maddening screech across the pebbles.

Elly was determined to enjoy herself. There were rocks to slither over and deep pools to investigate, but Ted said moodily, "The sea's too far out for a proper swim." He wouldn't even help Elly with a sand-castle, though she knew he could build the best.

He sat at a distance from his parents, who lay smiling at the sun.

So Elly left him and went humming towards the sea. She wished her dog was with her, splashing about. He would have loved it. But then Sunny was having a good time with Mrs Thorpe. Wasn't he? The mouse had said so. And with that thought,

Elly looked back at Ted. Where had he hidden the stone mouse?

She began to tiptoe across the rocks, but when she peered into the dark pools and watched the creatures that the sea had left behind, she was searching for a mouse.

The stone mouse heard Elly coming. She was singing to herself – something about a rose. The mouse sat, with his small feet still in water, enjoying the warm breeze and the song that brought Elly closer. In a few seconds she would be beside him and he would be safe again.

But Elly never reached the stone mouse. Someone stepped between them, blotting out the sun. A white shoe came out of the shadow and struck the mouse on the ear. He tumbled deep into the pool, his head ringing with thunder.

Ted was pleased. He actually gave a gleeful

little laugh. He considered himself lucky to have found the stone mouse before Elly. Perhaps fortune was on his side after all. What if she came looking in the pool, though? That's just what Elly *would* do. Perhaps she had already guessed that he'd thrown the mouse into the sea. She was investigating every tiny hollow. She'd be at it all week if he knew her. Elly never gave up easily. Without a doubt she'd find the mouse eventually.

Ted bent down, very quickly, and scooped the stone mouse out of the pool.

Elly looked up. "What have you found?" she asked.

Ted said, "Nothing."

"Oh, please show me!"

He thrust his hand into the bucket, pushing the mouse under a blanket of shells. Then, picking out the prettiest, he said, "There, then!"

Elly, stepping carefully over a bed of mussels, exclaimed, "You are lucky. It's a sting winkle. Did you know that? It's in my shell book. I've always wanted…"

"Here!" Ted shoved it at her.

"Are you sure?" Elly really meant: What's happened? Why are you being nice all of a sudden?

Ted leapt off the rocks. Wet sand splashed up all round him. "I gave it to you, didn't I? So take it before I change my mind."

"Thanks!" Elly watched Ted racing back across the beach. He held the bucket in the crook of his arm. As though something might escape from it.

Stabbed and buffeted by sword-edged shells, the stone mouse wondered: Now what?

*Smiling, Ted let the stone mouse drop down
into the dark earth.*

CHAPTER SIX

"The tide will be in now," said Mr Martin after lunch. "Ted, you'll be able to have your swim."

"I've got a stomach-ache," he answered.

"I've had enough of this," railed exasperated Mr Martin. "You're determined to suffer, aren't you?"

"Yes." Ted made a face.

"Well, you can get on with it by yourself. You're not going to spoil our holiday."

Mrs Martin said, "I'll stay with Ted. I want to write some postcards."

"You don't have to," Ted said in a more reasonable tone. "I'll be within earshot, at the top of the cliff. I'll wave to you now and again, if you like."

"I'll stay," said Mrs Martin firmly.

She went and settled herself at a big desk in Aunt Maria's cool sitting room while Elly and Mr Martin set off for the sea in their bright new beach robes.

Elly looked back anxiously to see what her brother might be doing. Mrs Martin waved from a window but Ted was nowhere to be seen. And then she spied him, moving among the pots in Aunt Maria's greenhouse. What was he up to?

When Elly ran into the sea she still wore a frown.

"Smile, Elly!" called Mr Martin, already swimming. "This is supposed to be fun."

"I'm afraid for the stone mouse," said Elly. "I'm afraid he's in danger."

From the grey stone wall, Ted watched the swimmers. Then he turned his back on the sea and walked towards a bed of white roses. He carried the little trowel he'd found in Aunt Maria's greenhouse, and the stone mouse lay in his pocket. His mother looked out and smiled at him and he gave her a brave, troubled glance, like someone with a stomach-ache might do. Then he knelt beside the rose bed, where his mother couldn't see him, and began to dig.

The dry soil gave way and Ted grinned with satisfaction. Soon he had made a deep hole, just wide enough for a mouse.

He took the stone mouse out of his pocket and held him up.

The mouse asked nervously, "Ted, what are you doing?"

"I'm going to bury you!" Ted told him.

The mouse felt dizzy. His voice dried to a whisper. "Why?" he asked.

Ted didn't answer. Smiling, he let the

mouse drop down into the dark earth.

"What is it, Ted?" the stone mouse begged. "Tell me."

"I'm angry. I'm in a rage." Ted picked up a handful of stony soil and when the mouse repeated "Rage?" in a frightened voice, Ted flung his handful down into the mouse's tomb.

"Wait!" called the mouse.

Ted made himself deaf. Scraping the earth with both hands he pushed it down, faster and faster, onto the stone mouse until the little voice fell silent. Then he smoothed the earth, very carefully, so that no one would guess what lay beneath it. But he found that what he'd done wasn't quite a secret after all. Among the clusters of white petals, four green eyes gazed out.

Ted jumped up. "Go away," he said.

Moss and Minnie stepped neatly from

behind the roses. "You shouldn't have done that," they hissed.

Ted ran into the house, slamming the door behind him. Mrs Martin called, "Is that you, Ted?"

"It's too hot," Ted muttered. "I'm going to my room," and he flung himself up the stairs, two at a time, in at his door and onto the bed, reaching quickly for a comic to hide in.

From beneath the roses, a voice called faintly, "Help me!"

Moss and Minnie scraped the earth, they dug until their claws ached and their pads were bruised, but they couldn't reach the mouse. Ted had buried him too deep. They rubbed their tabby faces in the earth, calling and listening.

But their friend did not reply.

Moss and Minnie sat beside the bed,
watching Ted, and waiting.

CHAPTER SEVEN

The sun dipped slowly.

On the beach Elly and her father rubbed themselves dry and watched the tide go out.

Mrs Martin had put away her writing and fallen asleep in Aunt Maria's comfortable armchair. Even the seagulls sounded sleepy. Upstairs, Ted flicked the pages of his *Beano*, trying to forget the rose bed. His head really ached now and his fingers were hot and sticky.

The cat flap rattled twice, but no one heard it. Eight white feet mounted the stairs softly, walked along the landing and turned into Ted's room. Moss and Minnie sat beside the bed, watching Ted, and waiting.

It wasn't long before he felt them, sitting close, breathing soundlessly, not a whisker stirring.

"What d'you want?" snarled Ted.

"You know very well," said Moss.

"Go and dig him up," commanded Minnie.

"What are you on about?" jeered Ted. "You can't tell on me. Now, leave me alone, I want to read." He covered his face with his comic but it was no use, the cats spoiled it for him. He couldn't concentrate. "Go away!" he cried.

They didn't budge, didn't even flick their tails, just glared at him; bored into him with a deadly, penetrating gaze. It was like being eaten from inside.

"All right!" yelled Ted in a fury. "I'll kick you out!" He jumped off the bed meaning to carry out his threat, but Moss and Minnie,

52

eyes blazing, spat at him and flexed their claws. And Ted found himself running from the room before them; found himself bounding out of the house and over to the rose bed like someone being haunted. And then he was picking up the little trowel, almost with relief, and digging, digging, digging while Moss and Minnie watched to see the job done properly. Hoping it wasn't too late!

Ted thrust his hand into the damp hole and lifted out the stone mouse.

"Ah," breathed the mouse.

Ted brushed the earth from the mouse's eyes and nose; he blew grains of sand out of the mouse's ears and held him in the sun.

The stone mouse blinked in the sudden light and said, "Thank you!"

"I'm sorry," whispered Ted.

The mouse and Ted regarded each other

for a long time, without saying a word. Moss and Minnie began to wonder if someone had cast a spell. And then the mouse, speaking very quietly, said, "I've been so frightened. Time and again I've thought I was going to be nothing."

"Me too," Ted confided. "You're nothing without a friend, are you? And my best friend is going away for ever."

The stone mouse murmured. "For ever? Are you sure? A best friend doesn't go away just like that, without making arrangements."

"Arrangements?"

"Without telling you where and when you'll meet again."

Ted, who had hidden his face in a hard shell, felt a tiny crack somewhere. "It's not up to us, is it?" he said. "It's *them*. Jon's parents. They're taking him away and *we* don't know when we'll see each other again.

They don't tell us. We were going to have one last day before he went. It was going to be the best day ever, with backpacks of food, riding anywhere, everywhere – just us. Something to remember. And then my dad says, 'No. We're going to Aunt Maria's; we've *got* to because she's going away and someone's got to feed her cats.'" He glanced at Moss and Minnie, who only looked at each other. "So I didn't even get to say goodbye and…" Ted gasped for air. His voice didn't sound the way he wanted it to, no proper words would come, just a painful, croaking sort of noise.

The mouse gazed at Ted's tears. "Poor Ted." He spoke very carefully, for he could feel the dark earth behind him, waiting for him to fall, but he couldn't help adding, "Don't cry!"

"I'm *not*!" Ted yelled.

Elly and her father, climbing up from the beach, heard a dreadful wounded cry strike through the air and bounding into Aunt Maria's garden saw Ted kneeling beside the roses. Mrs Martin had already reached him, but he didn't seem to see her. He kept talking through gusts of choking sobs that shook him in a way that frightened Elly.

"I tried to tell them but they wouldn't listen. I said, 'I've *got* to spend the day with Jon,' and they said, 'There'll be other days.' But there *won't* be! There *won't* be! Jon will be gone *for ever*. Just as if he'd died!"

"Ted, you've got it wrong," said Mrs Martin quietly, "it's only a year."

"A year is ages," Ted shouted. "We'll be completely different."

"If we'd known you felt so bad… Ted, Jon can come and stay soon, if you like."

But Ted just turned his angry face away

and muttered to something in his hands, "They don't mean it. They don't care!"

"I think they do," said the stone mouse.

"Ted, what are you talking to?" said Mrs Martin, alarmed by Ted's muttering.

Elly knew what lay in Ted's muddy hands and longed to reach out for it. "He's talking to the stone mouse," she said.

Ted didn't deny it, or call Elly silly. Clutching the stone mouse to his chest he ran indoors. And Elly let him go without saying another word.

*A door opened and Ted stood at the top
of the stairs.*

CHAPTER EIGHT

Elly sat on the stairs waiting to see if the old Ted would come out of his room, wondering if the stone mouse was clever enough to bring him back.

Moss and Minnie leaned close to her, purring like small machines. Elly put an arm round each of them and felt the tingle of comforting voices. "Is it over?" she asked the cats. "Has the stone mouse won the battle with Ted's anger?"

Moss and Minnie murmured reassuringly.

"I hope so," Elly sighed.

A door opened and Ted stood at the top of the stairs. Sunshine blazed through the window behind him and all Elly could see was a dark figure; she couldn't tell if Ted was still unhappy.

She wanted to ask about the stone mouse but she was afraid to. Ted might say something terrible.

He moved closer, down the stairs, one, two, three steps, over Moss and past Elly. He didn't look behind him but when he went into the kitchen his stride had a spring in it that hadn't been there before.

Beyond the kitchen door, Elly's family chattered quietly, then Ted's voice rose above the others. Was he pleased or angry? Elly had to know. With Moss and Minnie in her arms she walked, cautiously, towards the kitchen.

The cats stopped purring and listened to the silence that had suddenly fallen. Elly felt as though she was standing on the edge of a magic circle. So she stepped inside, and found her family sitting round the table. Ted was smiling.

The stone mouse sat right in the centre of the table, as though he were on a stage. The cups and saucers were standing back to give him space and he looked cleaner and brighter. A very special mouse. How could anyone have mistaken him for an ordinary pebble?

"Everyone looks pleased," said Elly.

"We are," said Mr Martin stirring his tea. "We're on holiday."

"But…" Elly glanced at Ted.

"Ted's feeling better," said her mother. "We've been making arrangements."

"Jon's coming to stay," Ted told Elly with a fierce sort of grin. "So you'd better watch out!"

"I don't mind Jon," Elly said and then, looking at the stone mouse, "I'm glad you found him."

"Yes."

Elly put Moss and Minnie on the floor, close to their bowls of milk, and then she joined her family at the kitchen table.

Mrs Martin passed Elly a cup of tea, and as Elly lifted it to drink she whispered to the stone mouse, "Thank you!"

The stone mouse gazed up at Elly and closed one bright, dark eye.